Storytales

Big Book of Monsters
includes:

The Return of the Jabberwock

Beowulf The Brave

MCDOOGLE'S MONSTER FARM
The Day the Gogglynipper Escaped

MCDOOGLE'S MONSTER FARM
Only Nooglebooglers Glow in the Dark

oh no!
Grumpy Monster is coming for dinner

The EATING MONSTER

The Return of the Jabberwock

Written by Oakley Graham
Illustrated by David Neale

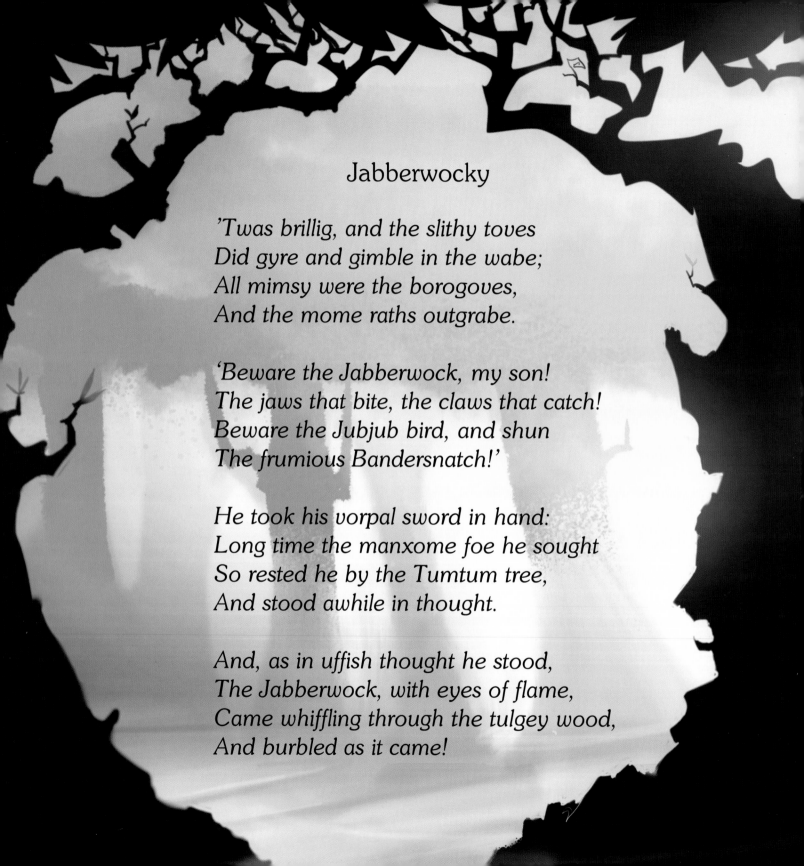

Jabberwocky

'Twas brillig, and the slithy toves
Did gyre and gimble in the wabe;
All mimsy were the borogoves,
And the mome raths outgrabe.

'Beware the Jabberwock, my son!
The jaws that bite, the claws that catch!
Beware the Jubjub bird, and shun
The frumious Bandersnatch!'

He took his vorpal sword in hand:
Long time the manxome foe he sought
So rested he by the Tumtum tree,
And stood awhile in thought.

And, as in uffish thought he stood,
The Jabberwock, with eyes of flame,
Came whiffling through the tulgey wood,
And burbled as it came!

One, two! One, two! And through and through
The vorpal blade went snicker-snack!
He left it dead, and with its head
He went galumphing back.

'And has thou slain the Jabberwock?
Come to my arms, my beamish boy!
O frabjous day! Callooh! Callay!'
He chortled in his joy.

'Twas brillig, and the slithy toves
Did gyre and gimble in the wabe;
All mimsy were the borogoves,
And the mome raths outgrabe.

Lewis Carroll, 1872

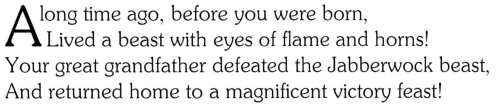

A long time ago, before you were born,
Lived a beast with eyes of flame and horns!
Your great grandfather defeated the Jabberwock beast,
And returned home to a magnificent victory feast!

'I'm going to find my own Jabberwock!' the little boy said,
As he marched past his dad towards the garden shed.
'I'll need a sword and helmet for my big adventure.
Then into Tulgey Wood I'll venture!'

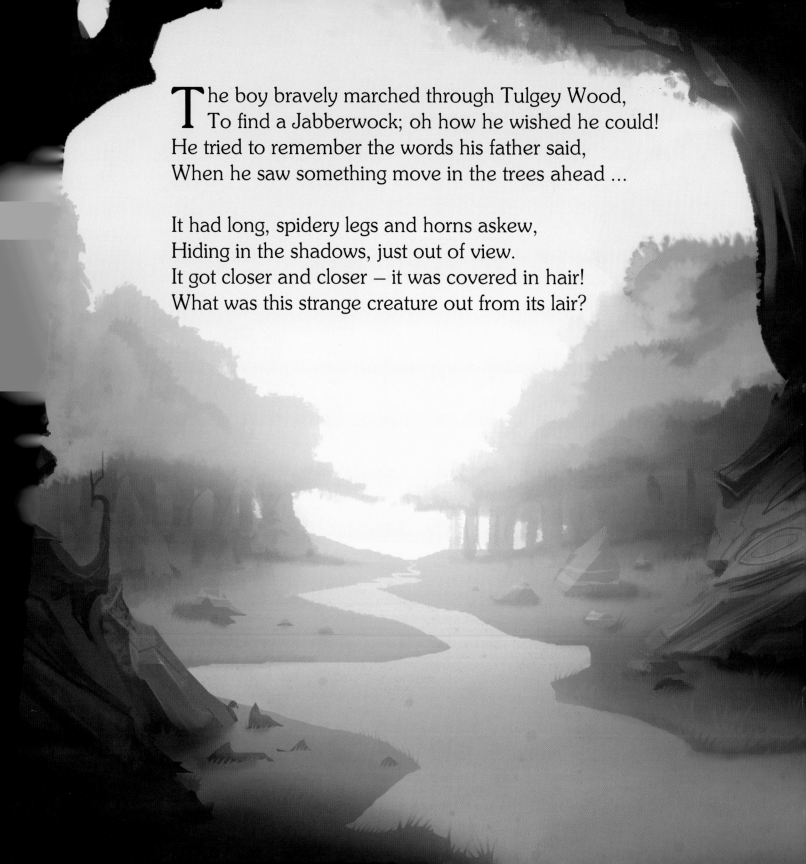

The boy bravely marched through Tulgey Wood,
To find a Jabberwock; oh how he wished he could!
He tried to remember the words his father said,
When he saw something move in the trees ahead …

It had long, spidery legs and horns askew,
Hiding in the shadows, just out of view.
It got closer and closer — it was covered in hair!
What was this strange creature out from its lair?

Then the moon peeped out from behind the clouds,
And a possum was revealed to the boy and bowed.

'Can you tell me where the Jabberwock monster lives?'
Asked the boy who was wearing a helmet sieve.

'Beware the Jabberwock! With jaws that bite and claws that catch!
Beware the Jubjub bird and the ferocious Bandersnatch!'

The brave boy continued on his adventure,
And deeper into Tulgey Wood he ventured.
Soon the boy was lost and filled with dread,
When a scary shadow appeared overhead …

It had an ugly beak and a toothless smile,
And it perched in a nest by an old sundial.
The boy started to tremble; the adventure felt real.
Would he end up as the creature's next meal?

The boy reached into his bag and pulled out a torch,
And shone the beam at the shadow, making it ... squawk!
A toucan was all that the torch did reveal,
Not a hideous monster eating snippets of veal!

'Why can't I find a Jabberwock to behead?'
Said the boy as he heard a strange noise up ahead.
Then a turtle-like creature appeared in the dark,
It had the ears of a hog and the mouth of a shark!

Just as the boy reached the monstrous creature,
Lightning lit up the sky illuminating its features.
No monster could be seen, just a pig in its place,
Another dead end on the Jabberwock chase!

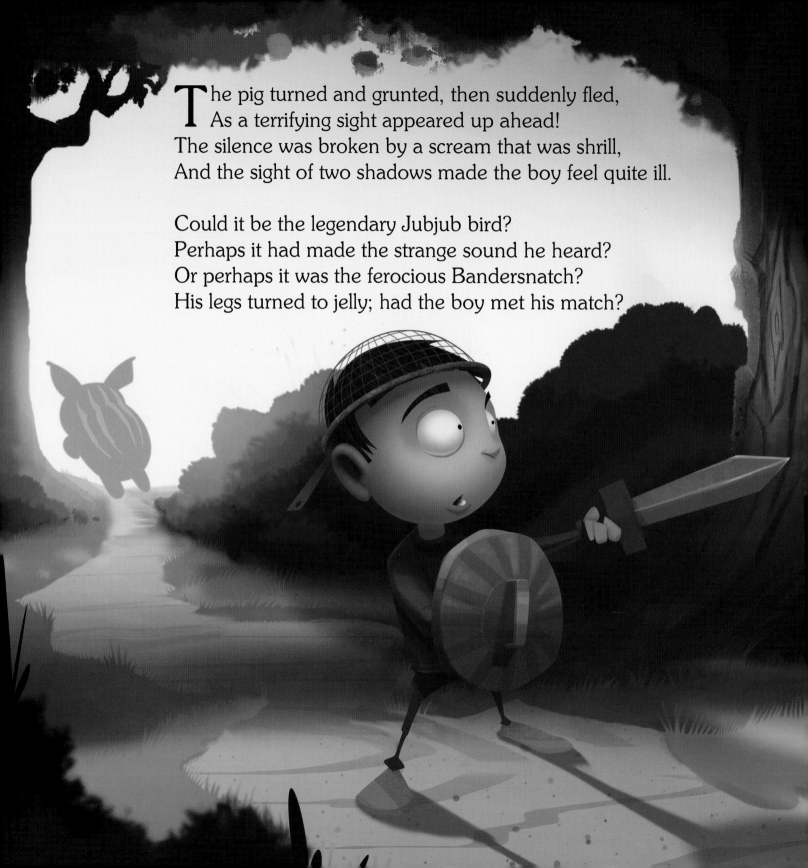

The pig turned and grunted, then suddenly fled,
As a terrifying sight appeared up ahead!
The silence was broken by a scream that was shrill,
And the sight of two shadows made the boy feel quite ill.

Could it be the legendary Jubjub bird?
Perhaps it had made the strange sound he heard?
Or perhaps it was the ferocious Bandersnatch?
His legs turned to jelly; had the boy met his match?

The boy held up his sword; not knowing what to do,
When the lights from a car illuminated the view.
In place of the Jubjub bird and Bandersnatch,
Stood a fox and a heron, stopped dead in their tracks.

The boy was getting tired; he was ready for bed,
And was starting to doubt what his father had said.
He asked the fox and heron, if they happened to know,
Where the Jabberwock lived and which direction to go.

'The Jabberwock lives close by,' the fox said,
    As he winked to the heron and pointed his head.
The boy rested for a while by a Tumtum tree,
And recited the poem of the Jabberwocky.

Then out came a creature with eyes of flame,
Whiffling and burbling from the place whence it came!

The boy took one look and as fast as he could …

... ran right back through
all of Tulgey Wood!

Beowulf
The Brave

A retelling of the epic *Beowulf* poem

by Oakley Graham

Illustrated by Emi Ordás

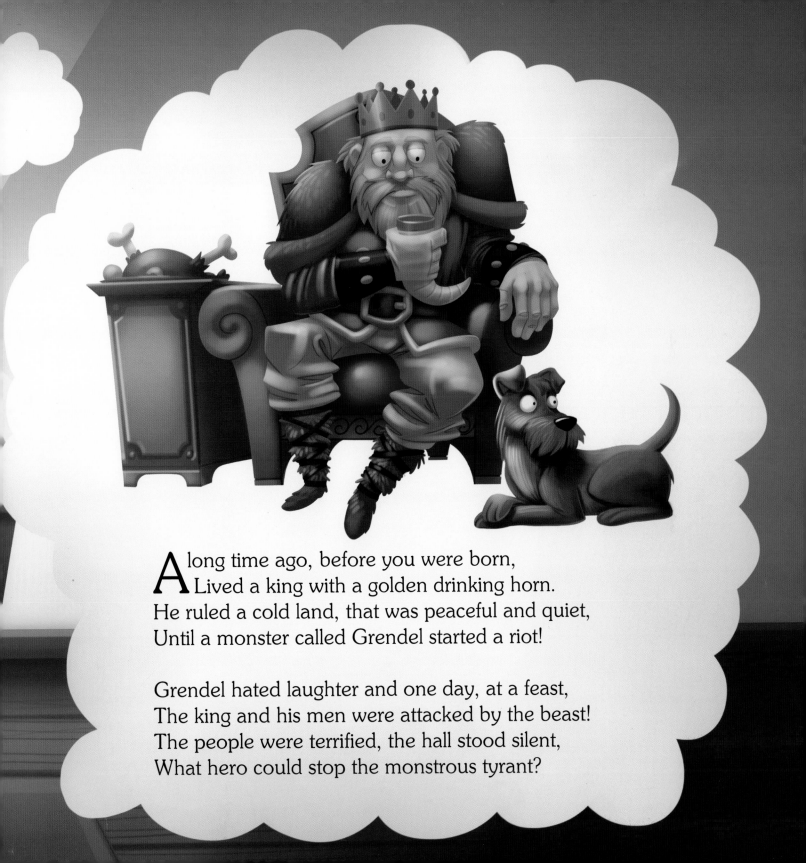

A long time ago, before you were born,
Lived a king with a golden drinking horn.
He ruled a cold land, that was peaceful and quiet,
Until a monster called Grendel started a riot!

Grendel hated laughter and one day, at a feast,
The king and his men were attacked by the beast!
The people were terrified, the hall stood silent,
What hero could stop the monstrous tyrant?

Then up stood Beowulf, Beowulf the Brave,
He feared no creature who lived in a cave!
His battles with monsters were legendary,
Remembered in song to make people feel merry.

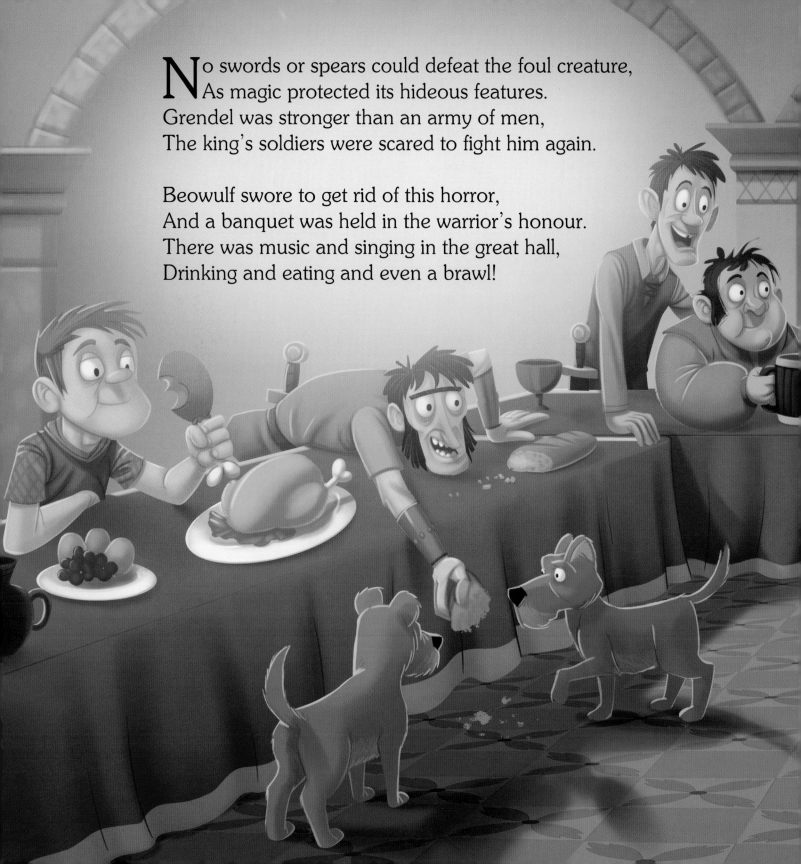

No swords or spears could defeat the foul creature,
As magic protected its hideous features.
Grendel was stronger than an army of men,
The king's soldiers were scared to fight him again.

Beowulf swore to get rid of this horror,
And a banquet was held in the warrior's honour.
There was music and singing in the great hall,
Drinking and eating and even a brawl!

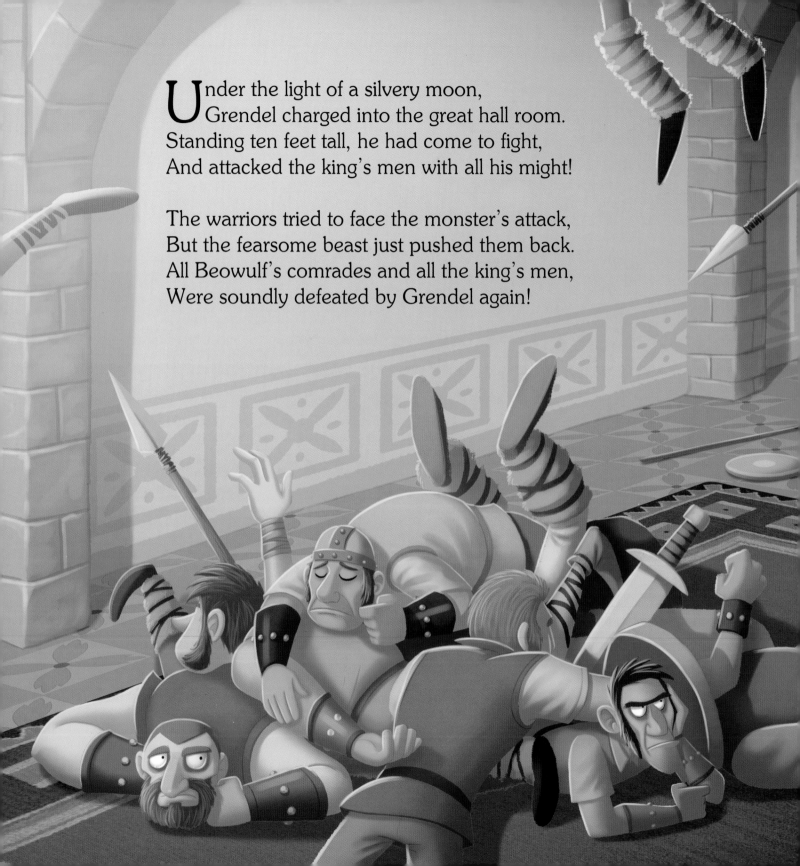

Under the light of a silvery moon,
Grendel charged into the great hall room.
Standing ten feet tall, he had come to fight,
And attacked the king's men with all his might!

The warriors tried to face the monster's attack,
But the fearsome beast just pushed them back.
All Beowulf's comrades and all the king's men,
Were soundly defeated by Grendel again!

Then up stood Beowulf, Beowulf the Brave,
To send the creature straight to his grave!
With no sword or armour, he launched an attack,
And knocked the foul monster down flat on his back!

Though Grendel had beaten all the king's men,
Beowulf attacked him again and again.
He fought the fierce monster, who tried to take flight,
But Grendel lay fatally wounded that night.

News of Grendel's demise was greeted with joy,
Except by his mother who mourned for her boy.
Now Grendel's mother was out for revenge,
And attacked one of Beowulf's very best friends.

So upset was Beowulf that his friend had been slain,
To destroy this new monster became his new aim.
He followed her tracks to her watery lair,
And with a giant's sword, he defeated her there.

Then home went Beowulf, Beowulf the Brave,
Across the sea on the ocean waves.
About his battles, the whole kingdom did sing,
And Beowulf was crowned as their new hero king!

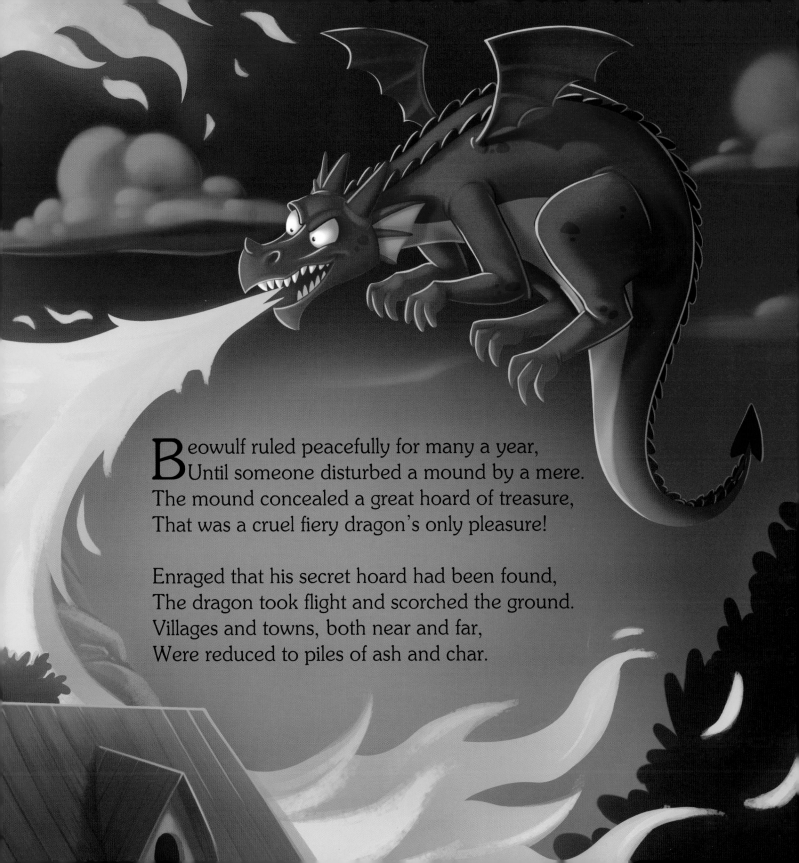

Beowulf ruled peacefully for many a year,
Until someone disturbed a mound by a mere.
The mound concealed a great hoard of treasure,
That was a cruel fiery dragon's only pleasure!

Enraged that his secret hoard had been found,
The dragon took flight and scorched the ground.
Villages and towns, both near and far,
Were reduced to piles of ash and char.

'Help us please Beowulf, Beowulf the Brave!'
Was the plea from every man, woman and knave.
'Your battles with monsters are legendary,
Remembered in song to make us feel merry.'

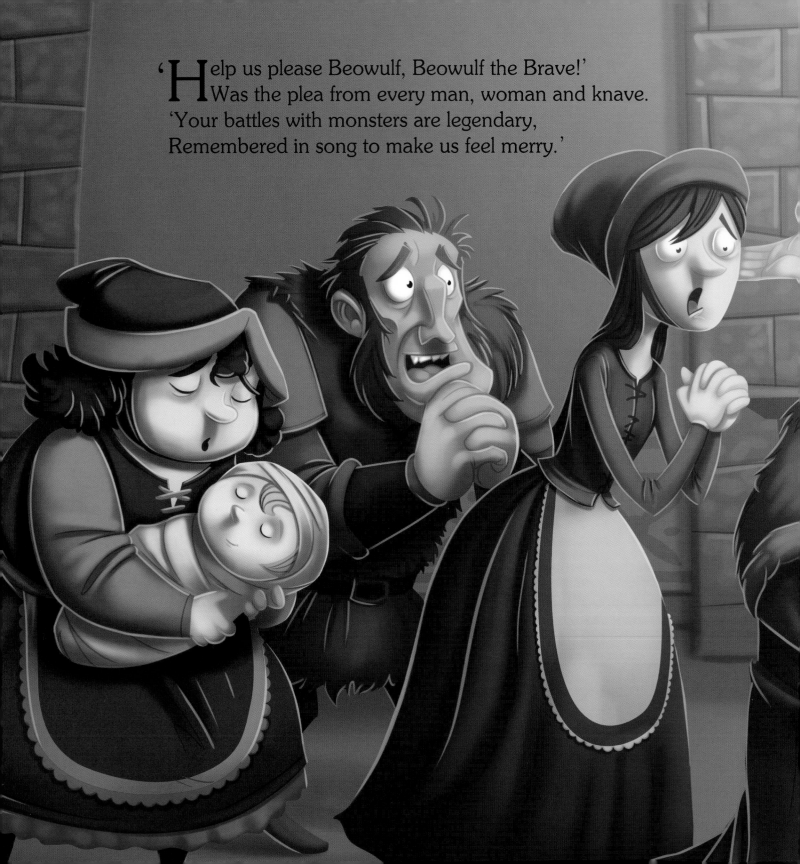

So Beowulf got ready and put on his armour,
To battle the dragon and end all the drama.
He pounced on the beast and rode on its back,
And drew out his blade and began to attack!

Over the castle and mountains they flew,
Fighting each other as the stormy wind blew.
Beowulf slayed the dragon, he'd won the fight,
But in battle he'd suffered a deadly bite!

The kingdom was saved, the dragon defeated,
Beowulf's brave feats were never repeated.
His battles with monsters were legendary,
Remembered in song to make people feel merry.

Beowulf

Beowulf is the longest poem in Old English, the language spoken
in Anglo-Saxon England before the Norman Conquest.

The story of Beowulf is set in Scandinavia way back in the 6th century.
It is a story of good versus evil, with the Geatish warrior, Beowulf,
saving his neighbours from a monster called Grendel, then defeating the
monster's mother, and finally protecting his own kingdom from a dragon.

The original Beowulf poem is more than 3,000 lines long!
The book you have just read is a shortened version and is written in
modern English, but it still includes all of the main action!

The story of Beowulf was told by word-of-mouth for decades until it was
finally written down around 1,000 years ago. Only a single copy of the
manuscript survives. It is kept at the British Library in London.

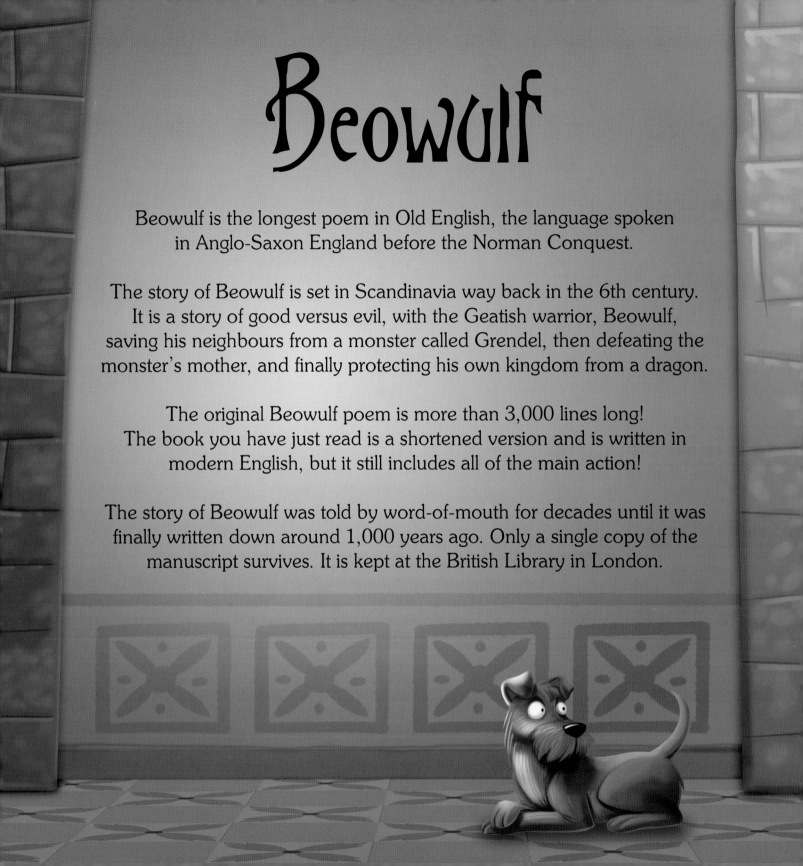

The Day the Gogglynipper Escaped

Written by
James McKnight

Illustrated by
Mark Chambers

One day, Diggle was out on the hillside blowing his special whistle, rounding up the Gogglynippers.

His trusty dog Noober helped him bring in all the Gogglynippers, rounding them up one by one, and herding them into their enclosure.

Diggle counted the Gogglynippers, 'One, two, three, four, five, six, seven, eight, nine ...
Only nine Gogglynippers! Oh no!' said Diggle.
'We're missing a Gogglynipper!'

How was Diggle going to tell Farmer McDoogle that he had lost a Gogglynipper, the biggest, scariest monster on the farm?

Diggle decided that he had to find the missing Gogglynipper before it got dark. He headed up into the hills with his trusty dog, Noober.

Diggle searched up and down the hills, blowing on his special whistle as hard as he could. As it got darker, Noober began to get scared, and howled along with Diggle's whistle.

Suddenly, Diggle slipped on a big pile of mud and fell onto his bottom with a squelch. 'Hang on a minute,' thought Diggle, 'this pile of mud smells very bad.' Diggle knew of only one thing that could smell that bad …

Yuck

… Gogglynipper poo! A big, steaming pile of Gogglynipper poo! A clue!

Then Diggle spotted some enormous footprints, made by an enormous foot with three enormous toes.

Diggle followed the footprints
into a big cave. He edged slowly
and carefully into the cave as
he knew that Gogglynippers are
not only the biggest monsters,
they are also the most dramatic.

Suddenly, there was a big, loud roar and the
Gogglynipper came running out of the cave.

He ran right up to Diggle, opened his mouth wide and licked him from top to bottom! (What Diggle didn't know is that even the biggest monsters can be scared of the dark, so the Gogglynipper was very happy to see him.)

Diggle attached a lead
to the Gogglynipper
and began the journey
back to the farm to
put the monster to bed.

Diggle could hear all of the other monsters snoring very loudly, even though he was very far away over the hills. (Monsters snore very loudly.)

When they were halfway home, the Gogglynipper started to act strangely. He sniffed the air and got very excited. Then he started jumping up and down, and began to pull on his lead. Diggle suddenly noticed a smell in the air. It was the smell of very smelly old socks. (Gogglynippers love eating very smelly old socks!)

Yum!

Yum!

Woof! Woof!

The Gogglynipper sped off in the direction that the smell was coming from. 'Noooooooooo!' screamed Diggle, as he was pulled along, hanging onto the end of the lead. Noober chased after them barking!

The Gogglynipper did not slow down for a second. He dragged Diggle up and down one hill and then up and down another.

Help!

They raced faster and faster!
Diggle couldn't even see what
direction they were going.

Soon they arrived back
at the farm. The Gogglynipper
raced straight past the monster enclosure,
round the corner to the farmhouse, and
straight up to the farmhouse window.

Hanging out of the window were two very large, very smelly old socks!

Just as the Gogglynipper was about to bite the two very large feet, they disappeared and Farmer McDoogle stuck his head out of the window! 'What do you think you're doing with that Gogglynipper?' he said.

Once Diggle explained what had happened, Farmer McDoogle laughed and said, 'It's a good job I only wash my socks once a week!'

Farmer McDoogle helped Diggle put the Gogglynipper into the enclosure with the other monsters, and they all went to bed. After washing their socks, of course.

The end

McDOOGLE'S MONSTER FARM

Only Nooglebooglers Glow in the Dark

Written by
James McKnight

Illustrated by
Mark Chambers

On McDoogle's Monster Farm, all the monsters have special gifts. You wouldn't know about these special gifts as they are top secret, but they are very important. For example, Gogglynipper fur is used as wire to hold up bridges because it's so strong.

Noogleboogler fur is used to light up traffic lights and Funderbiggler feathers are used to fill the sleeping bags that keep Arctic explorers warm.

Another of the Gogglynippers' special gifts is that they have the smelliest poo there ever was! Farmer McDoogle has a special machine that transforms the smell from the big piles of poo he collects from the Gogglynippers.

The special machine turns the pong into electricity to power the lights, the telly and everything else on the farm.

Once a year, Farmer McDoogle and Mrs McDoogle throw a big party for their friends and all of the people who visit them on the farm throughout the year.

To prepare for this year's wonderful party, Mrs McDoogle had spent the week making enormous pies and cakes with huge Funderbiggler eggs and enormous bags of flour and sugar.

The farm's helper, Diggle, helped Farmer McDoogle hang lots of decorations and clear a big dance floor in the enormous barn where the party would be taking place.

Mrs McDoogle laid out all of the food for the celebration and Diggle put on some of Farmer McDoogle's favourite music for the guests to dance to.

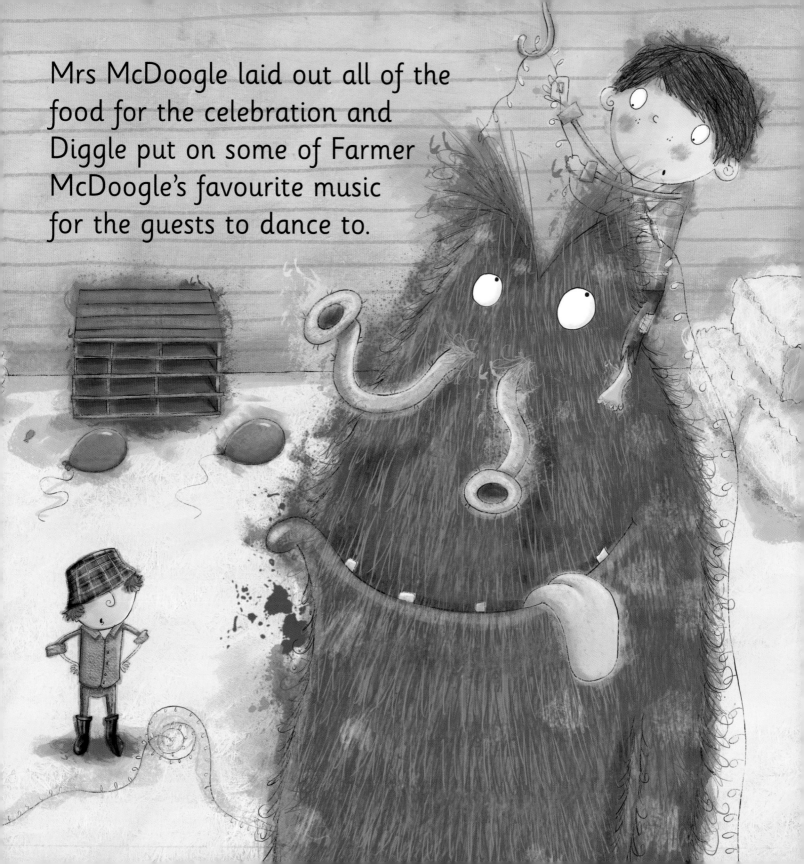

Lots of unusually dressed guests started arriving at the party, and some of the better behaved monsters were there too.

Farmer McDoogle, who was in his best suit, and Mrs McDoogle, who was wearing a fancy dress with a large hat, welcomed everyone to the party as they arrived.

The party was just getting into full swing when suddenly, the music went off and the barn plunged into darkness. Oh no! The machine that turned the Gogglynipper poo into electricity had broken down!

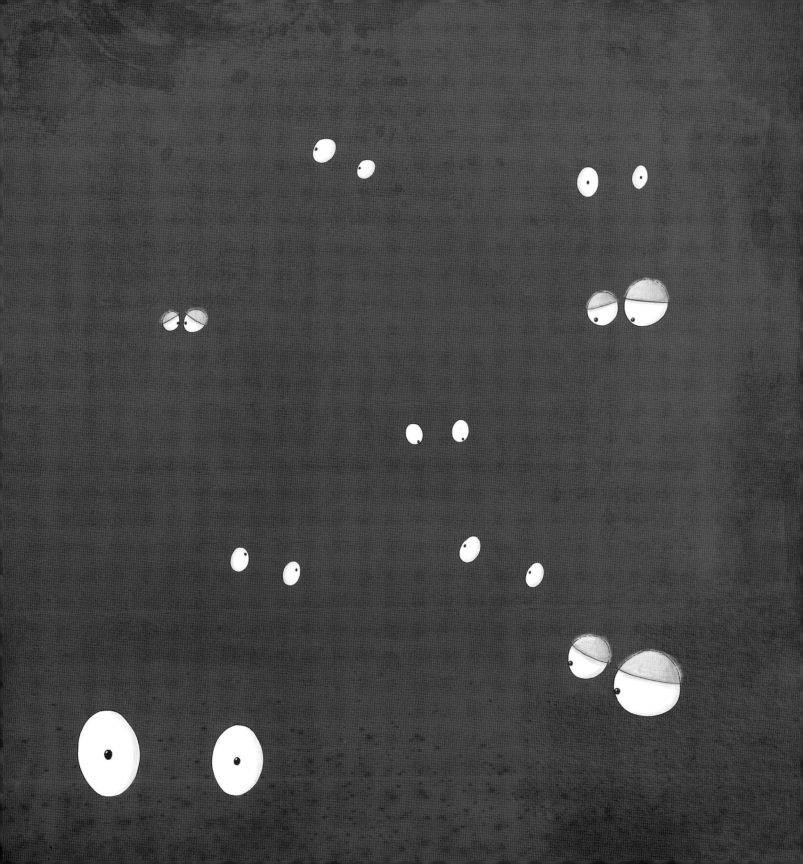

Diggle, who sometimes has the best ideas, had a very bright idea! He ran outside to the field where Farmer McDoogle grew the difflebug plants. Difflebug plants are very dangerous, but Diggle knows just how to handle them.

Under the bright moonlight, Diggle carefully picked leaves from the difflebug plants as they snapped and tried to bite him with their sharp teeth.

Diggle then ran to the barn where the Nooglebooglers were kept.

Diggle poured the bag of difflebug leaves he had collected into the Nooglerbooglers' feeding trough. The Nooglebooglers gobbled them all up! Nooglebooglers love difflebug leaves.

Diggle led the Nooglebooglers towards the big barn where all the party guests were waiting in darkness. The wonderful thing about Nooglebooglers is that when they eat difflebug leaves, after not long at all, they begin to glow in the dark!

As the Nooglebooglers followed Diggle towards the barn, one by one they began to glow.

Diggle led the glowing Nooglebooglers into the barn and they immediately lit up the whole party with their wonderful neon glow. 'Hooray for Diggle and the Nooglebooglers!' cheered everyone.

Hooray!

So the Nooglebooglers saved the party, and everyone had a super time. It turns out that Nooglebooglers have one more special gift; they have the sweetest singing voices, so made beautiful music for everyone to dance to!

At the end of the night, when all of the people and monsters had gone, one little Noogleboogler sat nibbling on the last difflebug leaf, glowing gently and singing his own beautiful song.

The end

Oh no! Grumpy Monster is coming for dinner

Written by **Ellie Wharton**

Illustrated by **Maxine Lee**

Milly ran down the stairs two at a time. She had seen something rather alarming from her bedroom window and she had to tell Mum as fast as she could.

'Quick, Mum!' she shouted. 'Hide all the china, hang the pots and pans out of reach ... Grumpy Monster is coming to dinner!'

But Mum was as cool as a cucumber and carried on cooking.

Grumpy Monster knocked on the door.

Milly opened the door just a crack, but Grumpy Monster pushed it open and bumbled in.

He tipped the hats off the hat stand, knocked over a vase of flowers and **crashed** into the kitchen.

Milly followed him open-mouthed.

'Do sit down,' said Milly's mum, calmly.

But Grumpy Monster didn't just sit down.
He threw himself down with a thump and broke the chair.

Milly's mum offered him a bigger one.

'Huummmphhh!' frowned
Grumpy Monster.

Then, 'Garummmmpppphh!'
he groaned, banging his fists down
on the table.

Milly couldn't believe Grumpy Monster's bad manners. But Mum just put a plate of food down gently in front of him ...

... and then another ...

and another ...

and another.

Clever Mum had made all of Grumpy Monster's favourite food!

He guzzled down
beans on toast ...

followed by pizza and then a meat and potato dinner ...

... then jelly and ice cream for dessert,

all washed down with a WHOLE jug of fizzy lemonade!

'BURRRRRRRRRRRRRRRRPPPPPP!'

went Grumpy Monster.

Mum laughed. Milly laughed.
Grumpy Monster's frown
began to turn upside down ...

He was happy!

And when Grumpy Monster was happy
he did happy things.

He danced the
tango with Mum ...

played hide-and-seek
with Milly ...

and sang karaoke
with them both!

But soon Grumpy Monster was hungry again and his smile began to fade ...

Rumble, groan grumble ...

Luckily, clever Mum was always
one step ahead.

'Quick!' she said.
'Show him the door, Milly!
I've told him it's time for
milk and cookies next door
at Tabitha's!'

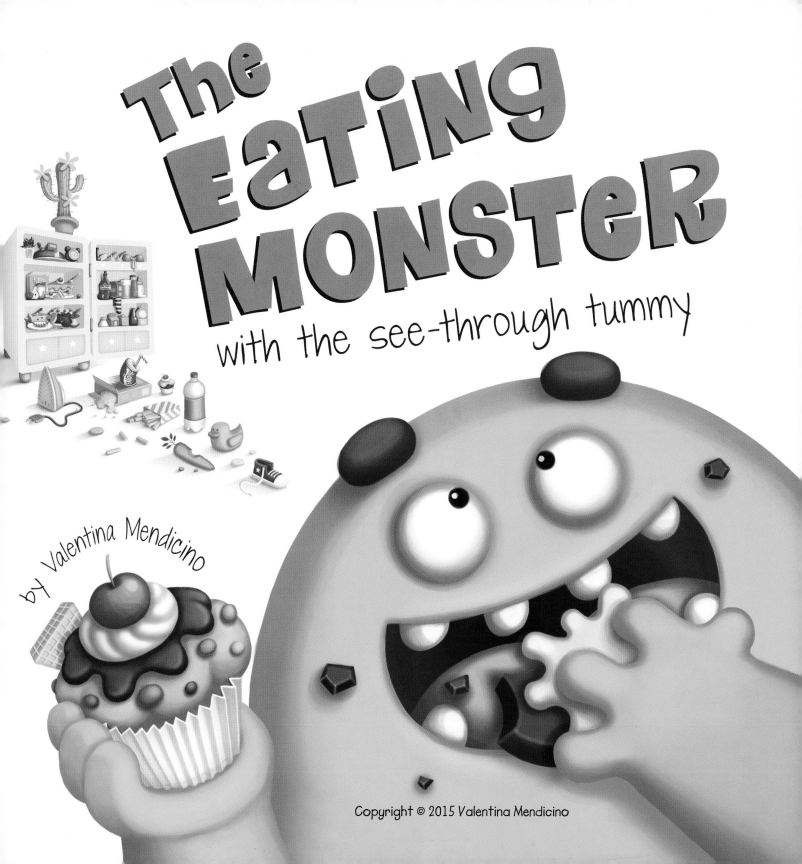

The EATING MONSTER

with the see-through tummy

by Valentina Mendicino

This is the Eating Monster.

He's not very good at reading ...

... or doing sports!

In fact, the only thing
the Eating Monster really loves to do is ...

One day, the Eating Monster decided to try eating new things.

This got him into BIG trouble with his neighbours!

The Eating Monster was ALWAYS hungry and the more he ate ...

... the BIGGER he got!

The Eating Monster ate so much and grew so big that ...

He couldn't sleep in his bed any more.

He couldn't tie his shoelaces.

Oops ...

He couldn't sit at his school desk.

He couldn't play hide-and-seek.

One, two, three ...

He couldn't ride his bike.

In fact, the Eating Monster grew so big, he couldn't even fit through his front door any more!

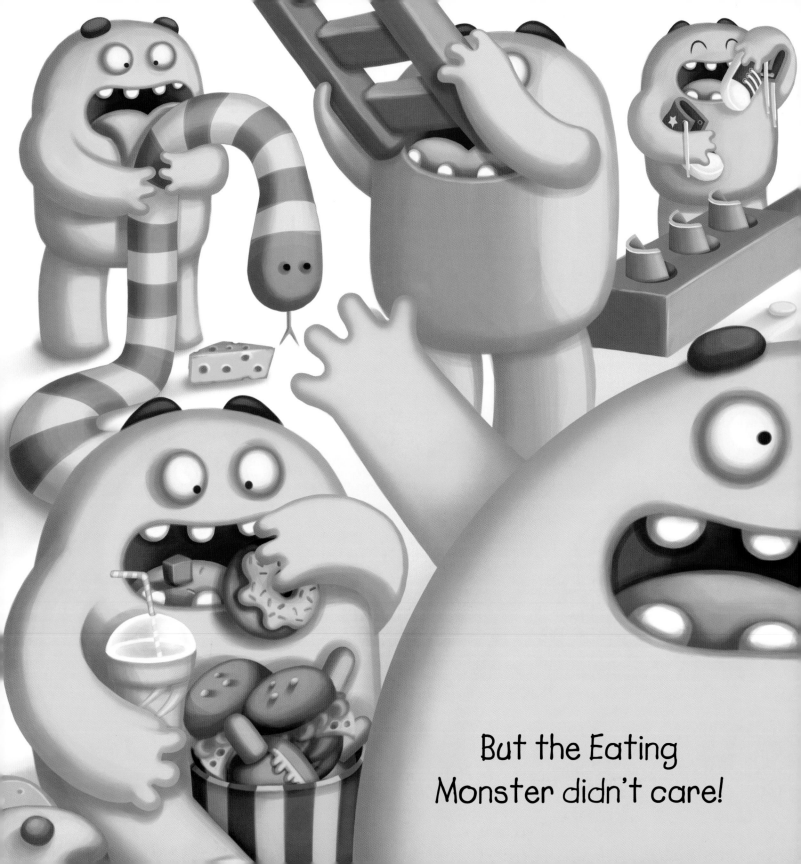

But the Eating
Monster didn't care!

He just wanted to eat
and taste EVERYTHING!

So the Eating Monster got ...

... AND BIGGER ...

... AND BIGGER ...

BIGGER

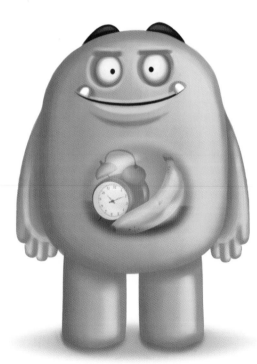

Unfortunately, as the Eating Monster got bigger, so did the things that he wanted to eat!

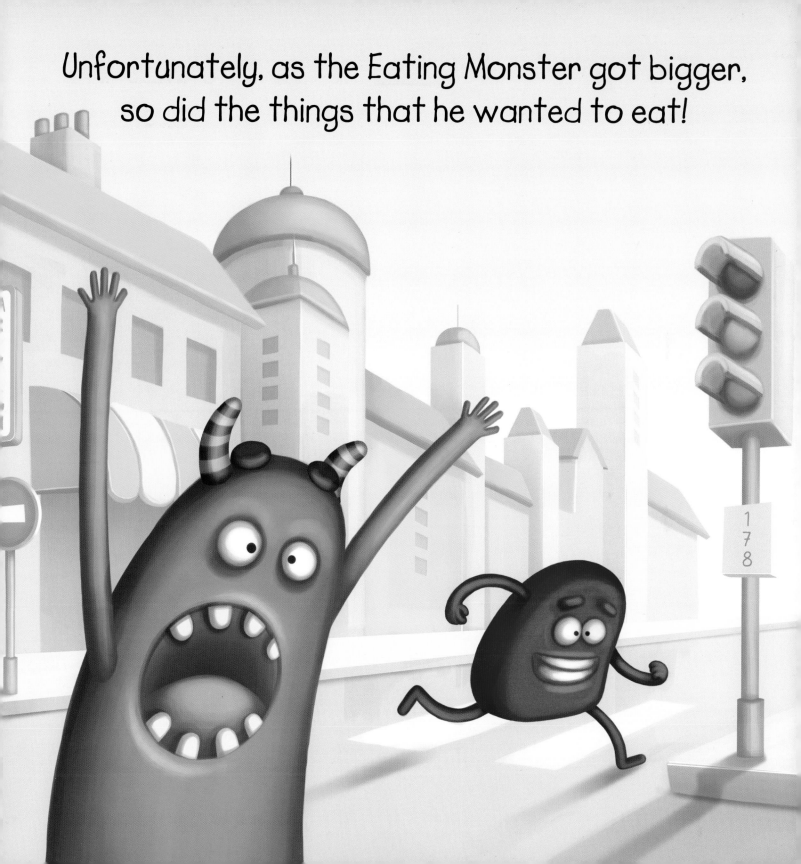

... cheese!

Even the Moon and planet Earth ended up on the Eating Monster's menu!

Soon, there was nothing left for the Eating Monster to eat.

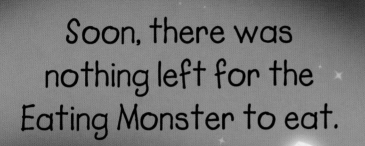

As he floated through space with his tummy rumbling,

Burp!